Poets, Prophets and Healers

An integrated approach to literature

Donald L. McIntyre

Words and Music
Gig Harbor, WA
In cooperation with Lulu.com

ALSO BY DONALD L. MCINTYRE

Books

Little Crucifixions   Songs of Sound View

Music CD's

Love Goes On   Songs of Sound View I, II, and III
The Bottom of the Well   Don McIntyre & Friends
Treasure in a Common Vessel
McIntyre and Eldridge in Concert

Other contact information:
www.wordsnmusic.com   www.donmcintyre.com

Meticulous effort has been exercised to ensure an absence of errors in this first edition, but such perfection is difficult in any endeavor. Reader suggestions for correcting the text are welcome.
Cover art - *The Calling of Saint Matthew*, by Michelangelo Meris Caravaggio (1571-1610)

.

FIRST EDITION

Library of Congress Cataloging-in-Publication Data
McIntyre, Donald L.
Poets, Prophets and Healers: an integrated approach to literature / Donald McIntyre. - 1st ed.
ISBN-978-0-6151-6213-3
       1. Literature - critical theories.   2. Christian
       Faith and literature.   3. Psychology and
       Psychoanalysis
I. Title.
809

to Angela Thompson,
healer

CONTENTS

Acknowledgments

Thanks to Abe Ravitz and Michael Mahon of California State Dominguez Hills, who oversaw the first iteration of this work, and much of the study that it reflects.

Thanks to Steve Brigham and Larry Burtoft, who reviewed the manuscript for errors of fact, and who improved the writing in several places. I still take full responsibility for any content herein that is inadequately researched.

Thanks to Kathy McIntyre, who supported in every way the efforts that led to this book, even though there were more than enough reasons not to.

Thanks to Heather Paul and Jason Asher, who read the manuscript 13 years after I wrote it, and encouraged me - sincerely I think - to publish it.

Thanks to Dallas Willard and Gil Bailie, who modeled and encouraged my search for greater Truth - not only beyond the usual boundaries, but also in the right directions.

Thanks to Steve Brigham, Charlotte Smith and Michael Pearson, my psychologist-healers over more than 25 years.

INTRODUCTION

The awful shadow of some unseen Power
Floats though unseen among us, --visiting
This various world with as inconstant wing
   As summer winds that creep from flower to flower...

      --Percy Bysshe Shelley, "Hymn to Intellectual Beauty"

Picture a technologically sophisticated Plexiglas chamber in which radioactive or otherwise sensitive materials are handled. To manipulate the materials, the laboratory technician fits his arms and hands into insulating sleeves, which in turn project into the chamber. Consider the components of this picture: the larger room that contains everything described so far. It renders the technician's normal or primary environment. However, in order to accomplish certain important tasks, some parts of the technician - his arms and hands, in this analogy - must function in a distinct secondary environment that is not altogether natural to them. They accomplish their tasks by a very clever means, utilizing a mechanism - the insulating sleeve - which is at once a shield and a tool. Please note the two distinct purposes: a shield and a tool. The mechanism shields the technician from the harmful affects of an alien environment. At the same time, it enables him to interact with that environment in various useful ways.

This is an analogy of human existence, specifically, the view of human existence that stands behind this book. It is a platonic and dualistic view of reality, contrasting with an Aristotelian and monist view that argues for no real separation between what I have labeled "primary" and "secondary" realms.

The intent of the analogy is poetic more than philosophical. That is, the picture has been offered not as a metaphysical absolute, but as a concept and a context that is worth considering.

The environment within the Plexiglas chamber is analogous to the environment of all our shared, routine human experiences. It includes conventional time, space, nature, physical relationships and physical actions; it is the realm of material forces and objects, ordinary consciousness, and conventional social interaction.

The insulating sleeves that are both "a shield and a tool" are analogous to the many ways and many means by which a person interacts beyond himself. Each of us interacts in and with the secondary realm without completely uniting with it, without emptying ourselves into it. The human body is perhaps the best example of such insulation. By closing my eyes or covering my ears, I can shut out some portion of the environment at will. By keeping silent, I can choose not to speak the thought that is in my mind. Likewise, my feet, hands and skin are all obvious examples of mediators, allowing me to interact with the world while also shielding myself from it. Thanks to my physical body, I am generally free to choose the extent of interaction with anyone or anything that is beyond me.

One other example of an "insulating sleeve" is language. When I use a word such as, for example, airplane, I am isolating a specific and extremely limited component of All Things. With one word, I call to mind a large, long, manufactured conveyance of human beings by air from one place to another at a remarkable speed. A word or phrase is a way of choosing out one small fragment from the Whole of Reality, combining it with other small fragments - other words and ideas - and considering these relationships as if they had their own existence, disconnected from all other things. Thus with words I limit how much of the world I will digest at any particular time; and in the same way, with words I limit how much of myself I will express. I have the power, through language, to insulate my ideas from those of others, and vice versa.

The Transcendent Realm

What remains for consideration from the analogy is the primary environment of the lab worker, the room in which he stands. In contrast with the environment within the chamber, this room is made for the worker. Its makeup coincides with the worker's physical needs and capabilities. The chamber - housing its unique and foreign environment - sits within the larger surrounding environment, the "normal" (that is, conventional and habitual) environment, like the fishbowl sitting in your living room.

It is difficult for many in the present age to imagine any human existence, any realm intended for humans, other than that which includes our bodies, material possessions, conventional human interactions, careers, institutions and the like. Our age is unusual in this respect. Human cultural history abounds in man's efforts to account for the sense of a realm beyond the temporal - a mysterious, transcendent realm.

The ancient Egyptian preoccupation with death and burial was merely one component of their preoccupation with this realm. Homeric Greece offered Mt. Olympus, and its philosophers eagerly explored numerous ways the seen is connected to the unseen. The *Tao te Cheng* teaches of an invisible and supra-rational Way, and invites its readers to enter this Way. The cathedrals of the Middle Ages were designed to invoke a supernatural realm. The philosopher Berkeley offers the extreme view that whatever is perceived as being "out there" is really the subjective creation of inward mental processes; and Emerson declared that "philosophically considered, the universe is composed of Nature and the Soul" (36). From supposed psychics predicting the future, to quantum physics, the spectrum of ideas about the unseen world is immeasurably wide.

The baffling variety of such explanations is evidence that the transcendent realm is vast and multifaceted. What is its nature? Where is it located? What does it look like? What sort of beings, other than man, inhabit it? By what sort of rules does it run? Such questions, if intended literally, only amuse because they attempt to treat the transcendent as if it were not transcendent. They point merely to how unaccustomed human language is to any but the most ordinary realities.

We communicate about the transcendent realm primarily through metaphor, as was exemplified at the very beginning of this introduction. A sincere smile on one's face is a "picture" of that invisible mystery known as happiness. A bicycle being peddled along the street is a manifestation of movement, the nature of which is more obscure than we imagine. A song gives expression to something called melody. The furthest reaches of outer space have always symbolized the idea of limitlessness or mystery. Thus, the transcendent realm and any of its components are conceivable to the rational mind by comparisons with ordinary, bodily experiences. Emerson explained the matter eloquently:

The use of natural history is to give us aid in supernatural history; the use of the outer creation, to give us language for the beings and changes of the inward creation. Every word that is used to express a moral or intellectual fact, if traced to its root, is found to be borrowed from some material appearance. Right means straight; wrong means twisted. Spirit primarily means wind; transgression, the crossing of a line; supercilious, the raising of the eyebrow. We say the heart to express emotion, the head to denote thought; and thought and emotion are words borrowed from sensible things, and now appropriated to spiritual nature...Every appearance in nature corresponds to some state of the mind, and that state of the mind can only be described by presenting that natural appearance as its picture. An enraged man is a lion, a cunning man is a fox, a firm man is a rock, a learned man is a torch. A lamb is innocence; a snake is subtle spite; flowers express to us the delicate affections. Light and darkness are our familiar expression for knowledge and ignorance; and heat for love. Visible distance behind and before us, is respectively our image of memory and hope. (48-49)

One of Plato's contributions to the Western philosophical tradition is his concept of forms, transcendent ideas or principles which are absolute and unchanging, and which give shape to all the changing physical and social realities of human existence. Twenty-three centuries after Plato, Carl Jung theorized extensively about what he called archetypes, by which he meant recurring patterns and themes in the collective unconscious of humanity. Though each thinker writes with a unique emphasis traceable to separate cultural epochs and personal interests, the proximity of some Platonic forms with some Jungian archetypes is unmistakable. In each case, something generally unseen but potentially discoverable is held to shape and govern the changing realities of human experience.

Three Angles of Vision, One Object

Since the transcendent realm is so vast, and since there are numerous angles from which it may be perceived, this book must place certain parameters upon itself. Therefore, only three of the numerous perceptive grids - Religion, Psychology and especially Literature - will be treated herein. However, each of these also is vast and multifaceted, each with its component traditions, schools and family conflicts. No one work of this or any other kind could venture to provide full treatments. For this reason, corresponding to the particular interests and objectives of its author, this book will draw from the Protestant Christian Tradition, Freudian and Jungian Psychology, and British and American Literature.

But the subject matter is still too broad. Therefore, what principle will decide my selection of subjects? Simply this: that there is an analogous relationship between the metaphors of literary, psychological and spiritual theory; and therefore, a synthesis can be achieved by comparing the different metaphors used by each discipline to refer to a given transcendent entity.

That sentence is rather dense and complex. The reader's understanding might be assisted if I unpack it a little. An orderly list of the main ideas might be:

- Theorists of literature, psychology, and Christian spirituality use specialized metaphors and terminologies that seem unique to each discipline.

- Nevertheless, the literary imagination, the psyche, and the spiritual realm are not mutually exclusive entities, evidenced by the fact that each discipline borrows metaphors from the others.

- It is reasonable to assume that each of the three disciplines has insights into the transcendent realm that are not shared by the others.

- If artificial boundaries between the disciplines can be erased, a synthesis is possible which would likely give significant insight into the transcendent realm.

Narrowing our intent a little more, the primary goal will be to formulate an approach to literature - a way of experiencing or "using" literature - based on some points of correspondence which literature has with both Christian spirituality and psychology. Though I can claim a degree of academic expertise in literary theory and the Christian faith, I confess to being an amateur in psychological studies. I would be eager to receive comments or corrections by those more knowledgeable than myself.

Examples from the Three Disciplines

"The Kingdom of God is within you," says Jesus in the Gospel of Luke (KJV 17.21). And this is merely the best-known statement of the New Testament's intense interest in a realm beyond common human consciousness that exerts great influence in worldly affairs. The apostle Paul speaks of the "heavenly places" (Eph. 1.3, 6.12, Heb. 12.1) in which resides angels, demons, the spirits of persons both alive and dead, and God himself. The writer of the book of Hebrews speaks of a world "behind the veil" (6.19, 10.20), interpreting the symbolism of the Jewish temple as a picture of a dualistic reality.

Such New Testament passages carry on the prominent Old Testament tradition of a secret realm. The prophet Elisha prayed that his servant's eyes might be opened so that he might see a portion of this realm (2 Kings 6.17). When the prayer was answered, the servant was suddenly aware of a vast army of angels on a nearby hillside on which, just moments before, he had seen only Syrian soldiers.

In 19th century Europe, in the wake of the diminishing of church authority and the Judeo-Christian worldview, the science of psychology gained a prominence that has continued and increased. With it came Freud's revolutionary doctrine of the subconscious, the doctrine that human beings operate out of a grand and in many ways frightening inner world of memories, desires, drives, feelings and ideas, most of which are not present to ordinary consciousness. Notwithstanding Freud's aversion to Christianity, the members of the primitive Christian churches saw one of the conspicuous benefits of the new faith to be what today would be termed psychological healing (2 Cor. 1.3-7, Eph. 4.20-24). It was largely in response to the church's decreasing effectiveness in this regard that psychoanalysis arose.

Spanning all epochs from Paul to Freud, and long before and long afterward, has been the ubiquitous presence of imaginative literature: poetry, myths, plays and, relatively recently, the novel. In the delicate yet powerful interplay between author and reader, as they meet together in the imagined world of the literary work, a very mysterious inward process is half observed, half invoked. Fictional characters, with inward consciousness and external troubles, proceed toward various objectives, through various obstacles. But both the experienced reader and the knowledgeable writer recognize that this is definitely not "just a story." Something profound and magical is happening within the reader. There is a hidden world that is shared by writer, story character and reader alike, and the history of that world is progressing as the imaginative work is perused. Thus does the creative imagination prove itself to be much more than just a faculty for making up things that do not really exist. Rather, the imagination is a remarkable way of seeing something that is really there. *Imagination is a method of seeing.*

Differences

The idea that these three endeavors - literature, Christianity, and psychology - are analogous in significant ways should not be startling. The reason for surprise consists in their customary segregation, and the animosity with which each is sometimes defended against the others' intrusions. Thus before exploring the many ways in which the three coincide, an acknowledgement is in order that they are, at certain points, mutually exclusive. It is obvious, for example, that Christianity has a far greater explicit interest in a personal God than the others. Some of the most helpful manifestations of literary or psychological endeavor have been frankly atheistic. Another contrast can be made between Psychology, which generally strives to be scientific, and the other two, which are often blatantly anti-scientific in many of their methods. A third example can be found in the fact that literature, even great literature, is very often acknowledged as being little more than a mere diversion. Whatever ways religion and psychology may be at odds otherwise, they clearly share the common conviction that they always offer much more than mere entertainment.

It is my contention that a remarkable number of differences are merely apparent - matters of emphasis, language or cultural expression - and that, notwithstanding the important work of Jung and the archetypal critics, there is still much to be gained by exploring the points at which they converge.

Convergence and Mutual Supplementality

As Matthew Arnold expressed in his poem "Dover Beach," different ages and cultures have their different emphases. To him, some ages were religious, some irreligious. No matter what the emphasis, the transcendent realm seems to remain a constant, and will continuously be engaged by one method or another. Thus, Arnold called for poetry to take the moral place of Christian spirituality in what he considered a post-Christian age. What Arnold expected of poetry, Freud expected of his psychoanalysis. What they shared - both with each other and with the Christianity they saw being eclipsed - was a belief in the transcendent life and the need to engage it.

If a simple Venn diagram comes to mind (there's another metaphor), the point will have been established. Many of the seeming differences between these disciplines present opportunities for learning, since the insight of one will often supplement another - once the analogous relationship is seen.

Oversimplification

Without a doubt, some of what might be called oversimplification will be necessary for the purpose of this book; significant nuances in each field will have to be put aside in the cause of the larger picture. However, it will not be unlike the "oversimplifying" which aims at curing racial prejudice by emphasizing common humanity. There really is a profound commonality that unites people of differing races; and there really is a profound commonality between these three endeavors. The client in the psychologist's office is becoming more conscious and alive by exploring his hidden psychic forces under the guidance of a healer. The Christian "disciple" is "working out his salvation" by becoming more conversant with spiritual reality under the guidance of the Scriptures and the redemptive community. The poet expresses with symbols a vision he has seen wherein some commonplace has been charged with profound, inward meaning. He does so under the guidance of his muse and the wider literary tradition. The reader, under the guidance of the author and even of the story's protagonist, experiences some unexpected portion of himself and his hidden life in the characters and setting of a story.

A devotee of any one of these endeavors, conscious of the unique glories of his own area of interest, will most likely chafe at such comparisons, and rightly so, if my intention is to collapse all the boundaries that exist between them. But though these are largely separate pursuits in many ways, the over-specialization that characterizes our age is not an unmixed blessing. The health of a culture depends at least in part on the ability of its various components to sometimes gather and compare notes.

One note of caution: It will be an unfortunate misreading of this book if the term "Christianity" invokes images merely of inquisitions or witch burnings, or unsubstantial television preachers, shiny offering plates, and hymns that are sung powerlessly for the sake of tradition, or missionaries who add the burden of Western Fundamentalism to poorly developed cultures, or any other image of one's humanity being sacrificed in the name of Christian "righteousness." Such images are unavoidable in a post-Christian world (by which is meant a world in which the institutional church no longer drives public policy). Nevertheless, a fruitful reading of this book must allow for a positive, albeit uncelebrated, Christian subculture, a version of Christianity which has only the slightest connection with the negative stereotypes.

Arnold described Western Culture's flow of ideas as being a dialectic between Hellenism (Classical Greek Traditions) and Hebraism (Biblical Traditions). This is in many ways an insightful paradigm, but the point must not be missed that the best of each was long ago synthesized and vitalized in that version of Christianity that existed in the First Century A.D. It has been to the great detriment of the modern church that it is too far removed from that primitive union.

Precedents

This book is by no means the first attempt to explore these connections. Precedents have existed for millennia. Indeed, one regularly observes in pre-classical civilizations a blurring of distinctions between ritual, the arts, religious practices, science, and primitive forms of social psychology.

There is some apprehension in the present age, especially among the educated, about whatever bridges may exist between Christianity and literature. Much of this uneasiness may stem from associations with medieval Scholasticism, and the constraint that was placed upon the imaginative mind by the medieval church. During that time, Literature - indeed all the arts - seems often to have been little more than the endless rehearsing of

Catholic doctrines. The extant morality play *Everyman* (ca. 1500) is an example, and Bunyan's *Pilgrim's Progress* (1678) reflects a Protestant continuation of this strategy. It may now be acknowledged that the Renaissance annulment of this unhealthy marriage profited both the arts and the individual practice of Christianity.

There is no artistic benefit whatever to be gained by making literature the servant of some particular philosophical, academic or social agenda, but it would be a mistake to think that the medieval church has been the only force that has used literature for such purposes. Examples abound of approaches that sometimes forget to let art be art in their eagerness to carry out various plans for social engineering. Orr demonstrates how such over-eagerness can remove literary criticism to too great a distance from aesthetics, even in our own day. Speaking of recent developments in criticism, he says

Black and lesbian feminist critics charged that most feminist criticism of the seventies and the beginning of the eighties was still exclusionary, even racist and homophobic, valorizing white, middle-class, heterosexual women writers while ignoring minority and lesbian writers and characters... In a similar way, Marxist-feminist critics accused much of the early feminist criticism of studying only bourgeois or elitist productions while ignoring the most popular literary and artistic genres or literature designed for the working class women, or ignoring the whole question of class difference and material conditions among women... (139)

Formalist criticism or "New" criticism, in which composition more than message is the focus, or ideas such as those of Walter Pater, will always have relevance because there will always be social agenda excesses; the church is not the only offender.

In addition, it would be a mistake to associate automatically a Christian commitment with literary mediocrity, even in the modern age. A continuing beneficial association of Christianity with literature has been demonstrated by the likes of Dostoyevsky, Auden, T. S. Eliot, C. S. Lewis and, more recently, Alexander Solzhenitsyn.

The psychological approach to literature already has a one hundred year old tradition. Freud himself can be labeled the official founder of this tradition since his considerable literary background nurtured virtually all of his theorizing and writing. Continuing the tradition have been the likes of I. A. Richards, who applied psychology to the creative process and the interactions of author and reader; and F. L. Lucas and Ernest Jones, who explored the "inner life" of fictitious characters. There is also the intermittently popular practice of analyzing an author's unconscious by means of his writings. And as recently as 1979, J. Hillis Miller was able to speak of a "powerful new form of psychoanalytic criticism, mostly imported from France" (174).

An important offshoot of the psychological approach is archetypal criticism, whose origin is associated most with Jung, but which is equally connected with Sir James Frazer's *Golden Bough* (1922). Northrop Frye is the most prominent critic in this field, and Joseph Campbell devoted his life to it as stated previously, collecting, organizing and disseminating myths from every culture. Its major tenets are that all human beings draw their psychic energy and broad psychological categories from a common hidden source, which Jung labeled the collective unconscious, that this source preserves the accumulated experiences, feelings and ideas of human evolution and history, that such content is maintained and made available in various constant, repeated patterns called archetypes; and that these patterns are expressed recurrently in all societies through rituals, myths and various other symbolic cultural forms.

Frye illustrates this approach in a well-known passage:

> In the solar cycle of the day, the seasonal cycle of the year, and the organic cycle of human life, there is a single pattern of significance, out of which myth constructs a central narrative around a figure who is partly the sun, partly vegetative fertility and partly a god or archetypal human being. (Bate 606)

Frye goes on to summarize the four parts of this "single pattern": First there is the dawn, spring and birth phase, which is the source of myths about the hero's birth, of creation and resurrection. This phase leads eventually to the archetype of romance and of most dithyrambic and rhapsodic poetry. Secondly, there is the zenith, summer, and marriage phase, which is the source of myths about apotheosis, sacred marriage and paradise. This phase leads eventually to the archetype of comedy, pastoral and idyll. Next comes the sunset, autumn and death phase with its myths of death and sacrifice, leading eventually to tragedy and elegy. The final phase is that of darkness and winter, myths about floods, chaos and defeat, and the eventual archetype of satire. Of course, the cycle then begins again.

Equally illustrative is Campbell's concept of

the *monomyth*. Monomyth is the label Campbell gave to the product of his efforts to combine and synthesize the myths of hundreds of cultures. In the monomyth, the hero begins by being lured to some threshold of adventure. He then journeys through "a world of unfamiliar yet strangely intimate forces, some of which severely threaten him (tests), some of which give magical aid (helpers)"... Eventually there is a supreme ordeal followed by a reward... Then he returns to the world of ordinary experience bringing with him some great help for its troubles (adapted from Campbell 245-46).

An excellent recent exercise in archetypal criticism has been contributed by the poet Robert Bly. His book *Iron John* interprets the old story from *Grimm's Fairy Tales* in such a way that it becomes a literary-psychological study of the psyche of the modern American male.

Wilbur Scott summarizes archetypal criticism's integrative role in relation to other critical systems:

It requires close textual reading, like the formalistic, and yet it is concerned humanistically with more than the intrinsic value of aesthetic satisfaction; it seems psychological insofar as it analyzes the work of art's appeal to the audience...and yet sociological in its attendance upon basic cultural patterns as central to that appeal; it is historical in its investigation of a cultural or social past, but nonhistorical in its demonstration of literature's timeless value, independent of particular periods. (247)

Applications

It is evident then that an interchange,

---

sometimes detrimental, sometimes beneficial, is already well established between literature and Christianity on the one hand, and literature and psychology on the other. Based on all the foregoing, a study that seeks to bridge the three endeavors could emphasize a call to contemporary Christians: You are no longer powerful influences in culture because of two deficiencies. You have lost your imagination, and you have lost the intimate self-knowledge which John the Apostle once called "walking in the light" (1 John 1.7). In this age, to be a disciple must involve a season of regaining these two lost gifts of God. You are invited to go in the name of Christ to the poets and the exposers of the psyche and discover what a boon they offer to your faith.

Or such a study could assume the form of a call to psychologists: Your pursuit is not as exclusively modern as you may think. Aristotle saw the theater of his time as providing the same service to its audience that you now offer: "Through pity and fear effecting the proper purgation of these [harmful] emotions" (Bate 22). Tragedy called up their repressed psychic forces, activated them in a safe environment, and integrated or purged them as appropriate. The Jesus of the New Testament was a healer of mental processes as well as physical diseases, as can be observed simply by an imaginative reading of his many conversations (as in John 3, 4, 8 & 13). And from pre-history to our own day, stories, poems and myths have confronted the subconscious and hastened its progress. If you leave behind such resources as these, you do so to the detriment of your own calling.

However, as I noted previously, rather than

pursuing a goal that is primarily religious or psychological, this book will focus on the literary endeavor, on some of the components of stories and poems that make them worth reading and re-reading. How is a poet different from a non-poet? How can some fictional characters create such emotion in the reader? Why do mere stories or poems sometimes have the power to change the entire direction of a reader's life? What is it about mere arrangements of words that make them so compelling? And why do some people seem to gain nothing at all from even the best imaginative literature?

Answers to these and like questions will be implied or explicitly provided by what follows; and at many points the answers are religious and psychological without being any the less literary.

CHAPTER ONE

Poet, Prophet, Healer

In vain we drive our stakes through such a haunter
  Or woo with spiced applaudings such a heart.
His news of April do but mock our Winter
Like maps of heaven breathed on window-frost
By cruel clowns in codes whose key is lost.
Yet some sereneness in our rage has guessed
That we are being blessed and blessed and blessed
When least we know it and when coldest art
Seems hostile, useless, or apart.

  -Peter Viereck, "Poet"

When Plato, through the voice of Socrates, was describing in The Republic the principles of his utopia, he took pains to limit the role that poets would be allowed to play in such a state, and why it should be so.

We must remain firm in our conviction that hymns to the gods and praises of famous men are the only poetry which ought to be admitted into our state. For if you go beyond this and allow the honeyed muse to enter, either in epic or lyric verse, not law and the reason of mankind, which by common consent have been deemed best, but pleasure and pain will be the rulers in our State. (Book X)

Plato rightly saw that the poetic influence would be as a gadfly - to appropriate Socrates' own philosophical self-definition - to his republic. If allowed unrestrained expression, the poets would likely stir undesirable emotions, and perhaps describe possibilities beyond one temporal utopia. The Plato of the above quote would have deplored the identification of poets with Socratic gadflies. Nevertheless, certainly the prophetic role which he rightly ascribed to philosophers in his own age would have passed to poets had his own philosophical dream been realized.

Earlier in the same work (*The Republic*, Book VII), Plato provides one of the great parables of the prophetic-philosophic-poetic character. Plato speaks of a cave in which people are bound to their seats, never able to observe anything of reality except their own shadows on the cave's far wall. Then one of the group becomes free and courageously ventures out into the bright world of light, color, living things and various sounds. In time, he must make the painful decision to return to the cave to share his experience, even though perplexed responses and ill treatment await him for his new and disturbing vision.

It is no injustice to this parable to say that it is applicable not only to the true philosopher as Plato intended, but to a wide range of true poets, religious teachers and psychological theorists. All these share one or more innumerable penetrating encounters with the world "behind the veil." Though they return with dissimilar word-pictures to describe that world, and though they apply their knowledge in different ways, the encounters of all take place in a similar "location."

The true poet is an individual who is connected in some unconventional ways to realities that are outside the commonplace. By some willful or accidental means associated with what we automatically call imagination, the poet is able to go to some source of experience that is somehow unavailable to the unpoetic, and then to return with an account of what he has seen there.

It is not surprising that the methods by which his visions are communicated are often as unconventional as the visions themselves. The uninitiated are a little baffled by the strange uses of language - the symbols, comparisons, synecdoche and personifications. They do not understand why the rules of grammar, punctuation or spelling are often suspended. In frustration, they may plead for the message to be delivered more plainly, and may accuse the messenger of being deliberately obscure. Indeed, mediocre writers, recognizing this complaint, sometimes make obscurity their goal in order to feign profound vision.

Those who are most captivated by the mirage of

the temporal may even wonder why stories, poems and plays exist at all, since works such as these exhibit no clear practical value.

The true philosophers, poets and prophets have this in common: They have a gifted - perhaps sometimes a twisted - vision to see beyond immediate, common circumstances, into the world of spirit, psyche and Platonic form. As Owen Barfield has observed, they have "extraordinary," as opposed to "ordinary," consciousness (211). This vision provides them with startling messages and unconventional forms of expression. It often alters their personalities so that their affect on their contemporaries can be unsettling. William Blake comes automatically to mind, as does the impressionist painter Henri Rousseau.

Still, it is worth noting that the poet is not an altogether distinct species. Rather, he resides on one extreme end of a spectrum. For as Emerson observes, virtually all human beings make some level of contact with the extraordinary:

Every man is so far a poet as to be susceptible of these enchantments of nature; for all men have the thoughts whereof the universe is the celebration. I find that the fascination resides in the symbol. Who loves nature? Who does not? Is it only poets, and men of leisure and cultivation, who live with her? No; but also hunters, farmers, grooms and butchers, though they express their affection in their choice of life and not in their choice of words. The writer wonders what the coachman or the hunter values in riding, in horses and dogs. It is not superficial qualities. When you talk with him, he holds these at as slight a rate as you. His worship is sympathetic; he has no definitions, but he is commanded in nature by the living power which he feels to be there present. (267)

Prophecy and Psychology as Poetry

The terms prophet and prophecy often mistakenly connote little more than the idea of foreseeing future events. But this is only one element - and certainly not the most crucial - of the prophetic ministry as it is exhibited in the Bible.

Prophesying, according to the Scriptures, is not primarily a prediction of future events. The Hebrew word for prophet, signifies one who speaks under the pressure of a divine fervor, and the prophet is especially to be regarded as one who bears a divine message, and acts as the spokesman of the Almighty...the prophet is the announcer of a divine message, and that message may refer to the past, the present, or the future. It may be a revelation, a warning, a rebuke, an exhortation, a promise, or a prediction. (Terry 405-6)

The prophet is a man or woman who, usually at God's initiation, is introduced to spiritual realities that are generally inaccessible to the larger community. In the biblical conception, God is trying to beckon to, instruct or warn the community through an intermediary. Use of such an intermediary is made necessary by either the unwillingness or the inability of the people to receive revelation directly from God.

The prophet then is a rather striking paradox. He is subject to all the same weaknesses, fears and foibles of his contemporaries, and is often not even distinctively moral or religious. Yet he is to be the bearer of the message, in many ways even the character, of God's invisible kingdom. This makes for some exacting experiences, and for some enigmatic methods of communication. Balaam, for example (Num. 22), has a conversation with a donkey, and must eventually confront the spiritual being that has frightened the animal. Hosea is instructed to marry a prostitute and thus become a living metaphor (Hos. 1). Ezekiel is instructed: "Get yourself a brick, place it before you, and inscribe a city on it...Then lay siege against it, build a siege wall, raise up a ramp, pitch camps, and place battering rams against it all around." (Ezek. 4.1-2)

Laying siege against a brick is clearly not ordinary behavior, nor could it possibly be used to communicate an ordinary message. It even bears a superficial resemblance to some form of mental illness. Or perhaps the resemblance is not always so superficial. In any case, some actions have the right to be labeled poetic behavior, attempts to use the familiar as a vehicle for communicating the unfamiliar and the profound. This is the poetic paradox. The other world, a god, a daemon or a muse is communicating itself through a mundane vehicle that in many ways seems ill-suited to the task.

Jesus carried on the tradition, showing the prophetic-poetic element of his ministry by telling parables about seeds and pearls, by writing cryptic messages in the dirt (John 8.6), and by using "figures of speech" (John 10.6). He even gave a name, "the Kingdom of Heaven," to the transcendent realm out of which he claimed to operate.

The psychologists for their part, with their Rorschach tests, their enigmatic descriptions of the components of human personality, and their hypnosis and guided imagery, show that they also function within the poetic paradox, finding their own unconventional methods for conveying an unconventional vision. Moreover, as Jung depicted in his essay "On Synchronicity," the transcendent realm seems willing and able to aid the process in its own surprising ways:

My example concerns a young woman patient who, in spite of efforts made on both sides, proved to be psychologically inaccessible. The difficulty lay in the fact that she always knew better about everything. Her excellent education had provided her with a weapon ideally suited to this purpose, namely a highly polished Cartesian rationalism with an impeccably "geometrical" idea of reality. After several fruitless attempts to sweeten her rationalism with a somewhat more human understanding, I had to confine myself to the hope that something unexpected and irrational would turn up, something that would burst the intellectual retort into which she had sealed herself. Well, I was sitting opposite her one day, with my back to the window, listening to her flow of rhetoric. She had had an impressive dream the night before, in which someone had given her a golden scarab - a costly piece of jewelry. While she was still telling me this dream, I heard something behind me gently tapping on the window. I turned around and saw that it was a fairly large flying insect that was knocking against the window pane from outside in an obvious effort to get into the dark room. This seemed to me very strange. I opened the window immediately and caught the insect in the air as it flew in. It was a scarabaeid beetle, or common rose-chafer (Cetonia aurata), whose gold-green colour most nearly resembles that of a golden scarab. I handed the beetle to my patient with the words, "Here is your scarab." This experience punctured the desired hole in her rationalism and broke the ice of her intellectual resistance. The treatment could now be continued with satisfactory results. (511-12)

Though Jung reports this incident with the disinterestedness of a scientist, its poetry and magic were not lost on him, nor evidently on his patient. They had received a visitation in this world that seemed to represent a different world. That other world had created an experience, using raw materials from the conventional world, and the experience had a deep and profound affect. These same elements are the crux of true poetry. A fruitless psychotherapeutic process turned fruitful when poetry invaded that process. A beetle tapping at the window just as a dream about it is being described - this is certainly a more compelling poetry than mere words on a page. Nevertheless, the fact is that countless listeners or readers throughout history have been equally affected simply by making themselves vulnerable to the poetic product. This is why Shelley can say:

Poets [are] those who imagine and express [the] indestructible order...the teachers who draw into a certain propinquity with the beautiful and the true, that partial apprehension of the agencies of the invisible world which is called religion... Poets, according to the circumstances of the age and nation in which they appeared, were called, in the earlier epochs of the world, legislators, or prophets...A poet participates in the eternal, the infinite, and the one; as far as relates to his conceptions, time and place and number are not... [poetry] acts in a divine and unapprehended manner, beyond and above consciousness...we are aware of evanescent visitations of thought and feeling...the interpenetration of a diviner nature through our own. (Bate 430-34)

Poetry Defined

It is expedient now to attempt a definition of poetry. This objective is extremely hazardous for two reasons. Poetry and reasoned definitions often have the tendency of impeding each other; and there are numerous definitions of poetry already, many of which have come from the greatest minds, all of which seem inadequate to most true poets. These appropriate concessions made, I define poetry thus: Poetry is anything that demonstrates the inadequacy of conventional perceptions; and in the case of poetry which is written, this demonstration entails the unconventional use of language.

A poet is one who draws his meanings from that other realm and lets its mysteries bend the language of his own communicating. Obviously then, there is much poetry that goes beyond mere versification. Good fiction may be considered a subcategory of poetry, and its authors as poets. In contemporary culture, a poet is as likely to make songs, comic sketches or films as written presentations.

The justification of poetry, if one is needed, is the same as the justification for Christ's parables or for helpful psychotherapeutic techniques. In all these cases, the participant is being challenged to grow beyond inadequate perceptions, perceptions that hinder the growth of the soul. Poetry is a call across a silent chasm from one kind of universe, life, or way of perceiving to another. The hearers, inundated with the mundane, are often at best only dimly aware of another kind of world, and often their ears are in tune for no other kind of music than the cluttered noise of busyness. The poet attempts to call to mind something concrete in the listener's experience, then say "It's like this."

The "inspiration" (*theopneustos* - God-breath, 2 Tim. 3.16) that is associated with Holy Writ hardly seems distinguishable at times from the inner energies that result in poetry. For poetry is, by definition, revelatory. It observes the same objects and actions that are observable to anyone, but it sees them differently, sees *into* them, sees their transcendent meanings, or creates those meanings - which for poets is another way of saying the same thing. To return to the opening analogy, the poet handles the "radioactive material" inside the protective case without disconnecting from the larger room in which the case is situated. Therefore, the poem reveals the glory (the value, the significance, the "light") or the horror of any seemingly common entity. The vision makes conventional language inadequate for the expression of the experience, as a perusal of Dylan Thomas' poetry or Joyce's later novels will demonstrate.

E. E. Cummings was known for his highly unconventional uses of language. Numerous examples from his poetry could be cited, but an even more convincing illustration can be taken from his prose. Cummings' unique style is not to be found only in his poems, because it was not just a writing style; it was a style of being:

I see people who've been endowed with legs crawling on their chins after quote security unquote. "Security?" I marvel to myself "what is that?   Something negative, undead, suspicious and suspecting; an avarice and an avoidance; a self-surrendering meanness of withdrawal; a numerable complacency and an innumerable cowardice. Who would be 'secure'? Every and any slave. No free spirit ever dreamed of 'security' - or, if he did, he laughed; and lived to shame his dream. No whole sinless sinful sleeping waking breathing human creature ever was (or could be) bought by, and sold for, 'security.' How monstrous and how feeble seems some unworld which would rather have its too than eat its cake!" (43)

Shakespeare provides persuasive insight into the poetic paradox with his characterizations of wise clowns in, for example, As You Like It and especially King Lear. Lear's fool is the wisest and most insightful character in the play. Very early on, he foresees the danger to Lear, whom he loves. His dilemma is disconcerting: How to warn a powerful and capricious old fool that he is self-destructing, without inviting horrid punishments upon oneself. The parallel with the Old Testament prophets is unmistakable. In this way, "clowning" is seen as a potentially very serious poetic activity, requiring great skill.

The application of the poetic paradox to literary technique is summed up in the phrase *transcendence in the commonplace*. Good literature will usually represent a convergence of, on the one hand, what Wordsworth called "incidents and situations from common life" (Bate 336) and, on the other, a transcendent meaning (as in Arnold's phrase high seriousness). Even Homer, who is not immediately associated with the commonplace - not even a Greek commonplace - exemplifies this principle. For even the dazzling and bombastic *Iliad* is largely about very human fears, marital conflicts, envy between peers, and a longing to return home.

"All things with which we deal, preach to us," said Emerson (59). The poets are here to help us receive the messages.

CHAPTER 2

THE INWARD JOURNEY

...Come, my friends,
`Tis not too late to seek a newer world.
Push off, and sitting well in order smite
The sounding furrows; for my purpose holds
To sail beyond the sunset, and the baths
Of all the western starts, until I die...

--Alfred Tennyson, "Ulysses"

My physical body is the central location of my individual will and power (Willard 53). With, and from within, my body I look "out" into a world that seems external to me. I notice and watch certain elements of it, I walk in it wherever my whim and ability carry me, then I touch, grasp, hold portions of it, modify it, use and misuse it, enjoy or recoil from the sensations it brings. It is a world which seems to exist independently of me but which I am equipped to engage. The equipment is my body, my center of independent consciousness that is able to mingle with that world without losing its discrete identity.

Aside from the fact that all this is literally true, it is also the best possible metaphor for a similar interaction that takes place in the transcendent realm. Just as I have a physical vehicle that equips me to explore a seemingly limitless physical universe, I likewise have some sort of psycho-spiritual vehicle for exploring a psycho-spiritual universe. As my body can variously enter into or withdraw from the larger physical realm, so my personal spirit can variously enter into or withdraw from the larger psycho-spiritual realm. Just as I may encounter other bodies, both alive and dead, in the physical world, so also do I encounter the spirits of others - alive, dead, imagined - in the transcendent realm. "Dead"? Of course. If nothing else, by simply remembering them.

Just as the physical realm functions on certain principles, entails certain processes, and contains certain categories of objects, so also the transcendent realm. Just as various behaviors will be nurturing or destructive to my body insofar as they heed or ignore physical laws, so also the personal spirit can be nourished or harmed according to the "rules" of spirituality.

This spiritual "movement" through a spiritual world is the reason Joseph Campbell has emphasized what he called *the archetype of the journey*, and this is why all great art, to the degree that it performs in a time sequence, depicts some portion or portions of mankind in process, moving toward goals. This journey - with increasing consciousness of and competence in the inner world - is a point of convergence common to religion, psychology and literature.

In Psychology, this world is labeled the unconscious or the collective unconscious, and the individual's vehicle for engaging it is called the psyche. Of course, this psyche is itself largely beneath consciousness. It is the central passion of psychologists to connect individual awareness to those portions of the psyche that are repressed or otherwise locked away, just as the medical doctor treats the hidden dysfunctions of the physical body. Once the individual psyche is more integrated and functional, it can experience fruitful adventures in a still unseen but somehow more accessible realm.

The Christian version of this journey has various labels for the unseen realm. It is a realm of spirits, or the realm of Heaven and Hell; the phrase "Kingdom of God" is used in this connection. Citizens of the realm include God himself, angels, devils, and the "spirits" of human beings.

Surprisingly, the realm is not only inhabited by the spirits of the dead; all people, even those whose bodies are still functioning, are said to reside there. There is "movement" in this realm: action, conflict, motivation, change, progress. In the unflinchingly values-oriented Christian paradigm, the fall was largely a separation of human perception from this realm. Adam and Eve "hid themselves" (Gen. 3), and people now "walk in darkness," "suppress the truth in unrighteousness," "will not come to the light," etc. "Salvation" in the

New Testament is clearly a process which includes revealing the hidden: a hidden Kingdom, a hidden God, hidden personal sins or hidden personal virtues.

No matter how different one's emotional reactions may be to Psychology on the one hand and Christianity on the other, their commonness beneath the terminology is difficult to miss:

- Separation from a deeper realm

- Lostness in one's limited perceptions

- The need for a difficult "journey" back to awareness

- The possibility of a more abundant earthly life

Good literature is a safe place to have a dangerous experience. It provides an environment that we are accustomed to think of as leisurely, entertaining, perhaps even silly. We tell our frightened children, "It's only a story." In Arnold's phrase, the activity brings both "sweetness and light." The light may be troubling, as in psychological counseling, but there is a parallel sweetness. The reader is free, if he so chooses, to regard the imagination as little more than a fancy, a harmless game of playing with the unreal. Thus emboldened, he dives into this "fanciful" world and there finds his own unknown self and his own unacknowledged psychic forces. In the words even of psychologists, he may "wrestle with his demons."

He may rediscover his own childhood environment in the Bennet household of *Pride and*

Prejudice. Because of the powerful emotions that are generated in him by this "mere story," the discovery is available to him that he still, in a very real and literal way, resides in that childhood environment. Yet, because this is so, experiences that in ordinary perception are frozen in the past and unchangeable are seen to be still present and dynamic. For though ordinary consciousness is bound by chronology, imaginative life is timeless - "eternal," to use the biblical term. He can now be strong where he was once helpless, wise where confusion once reigned. Perhaps for the first time he will learn to laugh at, and so forgive, various parental shortcomings. And in this way, the mere story will have effected something like a "salvation."

Or perhaps in *A Portrait of the Artist as a Young Man*, he will go back with Stephen Dedalus into the environment of his own formal education, eventually leaving that institution for the second time; but now as a more purged and understanding human being.

Or he trains his psyche for his own daily, personal battles - again in a subconscious way - by attentively reading *The Red Badge of Courage*. Or, thanks to T. S. Eliot, he can join the Magi on their journey, and begin to re-interpret and so accept his own painful losses as possibilities of new birth.

This is why I. A. Richards has warned his readers of "Irrelevant Associations and Stock Responses," and "fixed conventionalized reactions" (Bate 575). Such responses, as Richards rightly says, represent a "withdrawal from experience," and can only mean that the poetic confrontation has failed.

The stock response in literature is provocatively similar to what in Psychology is called *projection*. In both cases, the subject externalizes old psychic material on to an immediate circumstance rather than allowing himself the challenge of experiencing something new. One prefers the old, even if it is dull or obstructive, simply because it offers the comfort of familiarity. Such a reader is rather like Sisyphus, whose destiny was to roll the same rock up the same hill endlessly. This is the antithesis of the true poetic encounter, and it is the poet's duty and joy to "draw the reader in" to a real spiritual experience - to leave that old rock at the top of the mountain and go back down to retrieve a new one.

Those who study creative writing learn about the cultivation of believable characters, consistent voice and point of view, muscular language, stark imagery, attention to the rhythms of speech, integrated overall structure, and all the other "techniques" which are intended to invoke genuine experience. One of the mysteries of the literary experience is the real union it creates of author, reader and character. The literary work is an agreement of sorts between these three. In the transcendent realm, even the "imagined" fictional character is a real participant, having a real impact on real lives.

This individual journey is not always and everywhere the primary focus of those who theorize about literature. In the late 18th Century, most of English literature was dominated by a criticism that turned on classical models, and especially Aristotle's aesthetic investigations in the *Poetics*. There was a tendency toward inflexible rules of correct form. Plot structure was considered much more important than characterization. The individual creative genius, though he had been celebrated as far back as Longinus, was being unnecessarily restricted by ideas of decorum. The idea of imitating objective nature was more honored than the expression of the artist's own feelings and ideas. John Dryden had argued during the latter 17th Century for "refinement," "correctness," "propriety," strict unity, and simple clarity. These were the priorities of the neoclassic era. Alexander Pope (1711) is illustrative in both matter and manner when he writes "Those Rules of old discover'd, not devis'd, / Are Nature still, but Nature methodiz'd" (Bate 175).

The neoclassic rigidity, fed as it was by the scientific revolution that was then taking place, was bound eventually to produce a backlash. That backlash was Romanticism. Its first major poet was William Blake, and Samuel Taylor Coleridge was to be its greatest critic in English. The emphasis moved from plot to character, from correctness to individual vision and expression, and from the imitation of objective nature to the evolution of individual human nature. The creative imagination (rather than the classical concept of imitative imagination) became one of the primary foci of criticism.

It would be simplistic to assign to romantic writing some absolute superiority over neoclassicism. Excessive romanticism or romanticism without appropriate boundaries certainly does not produce great art, as is proven regularly in this country by hundreds of small poetry magazines. However, the counter-balance that the romantic movement provided in its particular era was both inevitable and indispensable. It corrected an excess that threatened the unique and exalted central role of literature as passionate guide for the human psyche. It is no accident that this included a return to the bigger-than-life protagonists associated with ancient myth, as for example, in Byron's *Manfred*.

The romantic era is an example in history of mankind's need for literature to reflect his own inward process; and not only to reflect it, but to facilitate it. Though the romantic movement as such gave way to new (and old) priorities in the Victorian era, its impact remains to this day. Nowhere is this impact more masterfully analyzed than in M. H. Abrams' *Natural Supernaturalism*, for there romanticism is seen as an adaptation of the Christian worldview. And the continuing romantic influence on culture is, in many ways, a "French Underground" in a land that has been otherwise conquered by secularism, science-olatry and despair.

Psychagogia

Literature has provided continuous and infinitely diverse models for instructing and encouraging the personal spirit along its path. It has demonstrated the need to begin or continue the journey, charted the landscape, pictured the intermediate goals, and warned of obstacles and antagonists. Most importantly, it has reminded its readers of their own spiritual nature and aspiration in those times when religion has degenerated into a mere formality deserving no sincere audience. Literature has provided poetic justice when no other form existed. It has produced epiphanies in times when The Epiphany could not be sincerely celebrated. It was "purging" the soul, according to Aristotle, in a culture that knew nothing of the Fifty-First or Thirty-Second Psalms. It was deifying man millennia before God became a man to demonstrate what man could become. It continues leading and persuade the soul (*psychagogia*) even in the midst of those critical theories (Art for Art's Sake, New Criticism, Deconstruction, et all) that ignore or de-emphasize its power to do so.

All dramas - Christian, psychological, literary - are variations on one essential theme: A being of immeasurable potential must overcome the internal and external forces that negate him, so that he may reach his noble goal. In Christianity, the ultimate goal is godlikeness ("godliness"), and the prime negating force is disobedience of God/conscience and the fear and shame produced by that disobedience. In psychology, the goal is the re-discovery and integration of identity; the primary negating forces are antagonistic introjects and the psychological defenses learned in childhood. In works of literature, there is an infinite variety of protagonists, goals and obstructing forces: Odysseus must return home, Hamlet must avenge his father's death, Jane and Elizabeth Bennet must get husbands, Eben Flood must come to grips with regretful old age, Gregor Samsa must create a new meaning for himself as a cockroach. But for the reader, the struggle is always a picture of his own psycho-spiritual (a redundancy) dilemma. Whether the protagonist is the lowliest of victims, as in *Great Expectations*, or a larger than life hero as in *Henry V*, it is the individual psyche that is portrayed, and the point is the same. The point is always to overcome the internal and external forces of negation in order to reach what can be termed, after Sartre, *authentication*.

CHAPTER 3

THE FUNDAMENTAL PROBLEM

He looks importantly
    about him,
    while all the spring
    goes on without him.

    --Humbert Wolfe, "Thrushes"

Aristotle provides the earliest known analysis of the fundamental literary principle of the tragic flaw. In Book XIII of his *Poetics*, he states that an excellent plot will show neither the fortunes of a supremely virtuous man turn from prosperity to adversity, nor those of the bad man turn from adversity to prosperity.

There remains, then, the possibility between these two extremes - that of a man who is not supremely good and just, yet whose misfortune is brought about not by vice or depravity, but by some error or frailty. Hence, in Euripides' *The Bacchae*, Pentheus fails to overcome his excessive need to control his citizens. Also from the pen of Euripides, *Electra*, because of vengefulness, becomes disastrously blind to her own shortcomings. And Sophocles in *Oedipus the King* portrays the power of arrogance and rage to destroy proper judgment.

Far from being applicable to Greek dramas alone, Aristotle's summary allows for wide application; and Calvinistic theology aside, it is an accurate general summary of the Christian view of fallen humanity. Predictably, it is also the psychologist's view of the patient. For each discipline, there is a compassionate but frank view of humanity as in need of rehabilitation from a fundamental flaw.

Though poetry, fiction and drama have struck out in numerous new directions since Aristotle, often modifying out of recognition the principle of the tragic flaw, they persistently make some fundamental human defect the focus of plot and character. All of Shakespeare's tragedies demonstrate the inability of their protagonists to overcome their tragic flaws. Ibsen's *The Master Builder* is a 20th century equivalent. In Shakespeare's great romances, such as *The Tempest* or *As You Like It*, we see these flaws being overcome. Jane Austen's *Pride and Prejudice* is titled after the flaws she is examining, though they are ultimately reversed and are thus not ultimately tragic.

The tragic flaw can be seen in much short poetry, such as Vachel Lindsay's "The Leaden-Eyed" or Lawrence Durrell's "Ballad of the Good Lord Nelson." Dickinson's "Success is Counted Sweetest" can easily be read as a wild lamentation (called a *Commos* in Aristotle's *Poetics*, Book 12) from some unwritten Classical.

Tragic Flaw, Mental Illness, Sin

When one discovers how much essential agreement there is beneath the rhetorical surface of our three disciplines, one is astounded that there is such a wide range of emotional responses to the words tragic flaw, mental illness and sin. The phrase tragic flaw connotes an academic consideration of what generates "fear and pity" (Aristotle) in the audience. Mental illness invokes a spectrum of images from "Eleanor Rigby" to the drooling, gown-clad, blank-staring occupants of an asylum. Sin, depending on one's past and present religious experience, calls to mind anything from one's own feeling of shame exploited by religious leaders, to the wrath of a holy God offended by willful disobedience.

A closer look reveals that each largely looks from a different angle at a common inward (perception of a?) problem. Sin is a basic destructive element in "the heart" that offends "the Father" and one's own conscience. Mental illness is an aversion, because of the fear of pain, to the fullness of human experience, and is associated with various "defense mechanisms." The tragic flaw is a potentially disastrous habit that must be overcome.

It is clear, once we notice the differing emphases, that each concept completes certain deficiencies in the other two. Sin is also an aversion to "the abundant life" (John 10.10) and must be "overcome" (Rom. 8.37). Mental illness is also offensive, for it is this revulsion to one's own neuroses that often gives one the courage to seek professional treatment. One is "saved" from sin, and "cured" of mental illness. The tragic flaw gains its dramatic power from the fact that it creates a certain repugnance in the audience, along with compassion and the hope of "redemption."

When people are confronted with the fundamental human problem, their images of mental patients or inquisitors, far from being harmless in their shallowness, hide deep truths, as is evidenced by a consideration of these religious-psychological-literary commonalities: In the midst of its excellencies and noble accomplishments, all humankind really does seem to share a common malady, an infestation in the soul, a disease, a corruption, a proclivity for self-destruction, a willfulness toward unhappy directions. In addition, all mankind seems to share an alarming willingness to cover its malady, pretend otherwise, and avoid "the light." "A man is a god in ruins," says Emerson (77).

To be sure, the malady translates itself into different individual styles according to individual dispositions. It is greed in one place, cruelty in another, gross deception in another, manipulation in another, and so on. Some version of the monkey seems to be on everyone's back, not to mention the backs of social movements, causes, governments, nations, and religions.

In the psychological milieu, the problem is traced to man's unwillingness to confront painful necessities - memories of suffering, and the affects of trauma. As Jung stated it, "neurosis is always a substitute for legitimate suffering" (qtd. in Peck, Road, 17). "Defense mechanisms" are built up by the psyche to keep out the sorrow. But these mechanisms also keep out much that nurtures and corrects, creating more sorrows, which then lead to more and greater defense mechanisms, and so on. The personality tends to become fragmented, losing its center, one component part distrusting another.

In his *People of the Lie*, M. Scott Peck has published a courageous attempt to link this process with religion's concept of evil. However, the idea is hardly a recent one, since the Apostle Paul once described his ministry as being one of breaking down "fortresses" (2 Cor. 10.4).

A chief methodology of psychology in dealing with the essential human problem is to collect case studies that may then be analyzed and compared scientifically. A chief methodology of Christianity is to compare one's own "case study" with those of the Bible and the larger community. The task of impressing the matter powerfully on the imagination is left primarily to imaginative literature. The arts are a relatively safe environment in which to confront vivid expressions of the human condition. Jesus knew this when he taught in parables. The inner person is enabled, not only to observe, but to actually experience, its own dramas, its own conflicts of values, its own tragedies, its own choices and possibilities, and its own deliverance.

Subcategories of the Problem

The resemblance extends into minute details. In Christian theology, the effect of the fall in Eden is sub-categorized into four forms of enmity: against one's own essential nature, against other people, against the created world, and especially against God. Psychology replaces the concept of "enmity" with that of "isolation." Again, the isolation is seen to be in the directions of the essential "self," human relationships, the physical environment, and whatever higher authority one conceives.

Literature follows suit, especially in its most stylized manifestations. In the article entitled "Conflict" in the *Writer's Encyclopedia*, five categories of plot-driving literary conflict are discussed: Man against himself, man against man, man against nature or environment, and man against machine - the latter being the only deviation from the theological and psychological categories.

In all cases, the core conflict is that which arises between component parts of the psyche of the individual, whether that individual be a follower of Christ, a psychological patient, a protagonist, or the reader of a story. It is these crises that provide a framework for the soul to make its decisions - decisions that will determine whether or not a given "flaw" will ultimately be "tragic."

CHAPTER 4

ORDER OUT OF DISORDER

No one can know how glad I am to find
On any sheet the least display of mind.

--Robert Frost, "A Considerable Speck"

All manifestations of life include order and organization, and all dying is a surrender to entropy - a journey into disorder and shapelessness. The human body is a systematic ordering of materials. In biblical language, the body comes from "the dust from the ground" (Gen. 2.7) and shall "return to dust" (Gen. 3.19). In the meantime, that dust has risen up and taken a definite shape according to a system of organization. In like manner are social institutions - businesses, churches, schools - manifestations of life, for an institution draws specific people out of "the masses," and organizes them in pursuit of a defined goal. To function is to create order.

Mental life also fits the criterion, creating an order out of chaos. Mental life reaches into the elusive, amorphous All, and separates and withdraws only certain portions. Those portions are then analyzed, compared, and formed into a new "body" with its own structure. Botanical systemization or the Calculus are obvious examples; a plan for place settings at a dinner party is less obvious, more mundane, but just as "life-like." Poems are various arrangements of once-amorphous materials, as are houses, theories of government and meeting agendas. Life organizes.

Ernst Cassirer, in his *Essay on Man*, observes that on the one hand human experience is astoundingly diverse, varicolored, multi-directional, and often even contradictory. Yet he believes strongly in the possibility and validity of systemization. There is a form in all matter, and it can be found - if nowhere else - in the analyzing, symbol-making, concept-creating mind of man.

And just as all life involves organized structure, all death is a loss of the created order. There is a death principle that is the exact converse of the principles of life. Entropy pervades existence. All biological movement ends in soil, the universe itself is moving toward dissolution, and societies, as Oswald Spengler described them in his *Decline of the West*, follow a life cycle that culminates either in being conquered (swallowed up in a more powerful order) or simply self-destructing. Human beings, no matter what they accomplish, no matter how eagerly they nurture their lives, are all destined for the same physical (at least) demise.

The seed is the best possible metaphor of that force in man that works against the death principle. The soil that surrounds the seed is an amorphous substance, a mass of chemicals and properties waiting to be organized. The seed contains the organizing principle. An acorn and an apple core will produce starkly different results out of the same soil because they will organize the identical matter in different ways. So also will two people perceive the same entity differently, and organize those perceptions according to dissimilar mental structures. So all life - physical, social, intellectual, psycho-spiritual - consists of a created order that starts with a literal or figurative seed.

The first act of the God of the Bible (Gen. 1) is a creative one, a forming of amorphous - "formless and void" - materials into an order which functions toward a planned purpose. This act of creation is accomplished by the speaking of words. The words, "Let there be" carried enormous productive power. Later on, man is created "in his image." The poet demonstrates that part of this shared image in his capability for creating new realities by the use of words, by saying in effect, "let there be."

One of the problems that the psychologist typically encounters is the patient's seeming inability to give some organization to his inner dynamics, or even to notice that they are in a state of disarray. Every significant life experience calls up an imposing jumble of (largely unconscious) associations and reactions that can only lead to dysfunctionality until they are consciously confronted and given an order. This inner confusion is usually reflected in disturbances in practical affairs. The patient may be unable to juggle (by organizing) the many demands of his job; or he may be overwhelmed by the many dynamics of any but the shallowest interpersonal relationships; or his home may be characterized by excessive clutter and disorder. All such troubles indicate a surrender to the death principle. And psychology looks for the root of such problems in the inability of the inner life to organize itself. Freud describes

...The procedure of construction whereby the analyst takes the raw material he has elicited from the patient - fragments, ideas, feelings - translates them back into evidence of the repressed material and puts it all together as a coherent story, account, or narrative, " a picture of the patient's forgotten years that shall be alike trustworthy and in all essential respects complete" (J. H. Miller 247)

Fragmentation and Poetry

The theology of the creative word and the practice of psychological re-construction are comparable both to each other and to poetry. One way of describing poetry is that it calls fragmented human perception back to its own order, back to union and unity. The ordinary human perceptive process is surprisingly fragmented and out of focus. It is endlessly lost in details and exigencies, often separating when it should combine, pressing together where it should discriminate. The poetic muse issues forth from a deep inner source of human dialogue, a place of immeasurable space and complexity, but that muse has a way of compressing that boundlessness into a comprehensible object, an organized creation, a microcosm.

- Fragmentation is indecisive because of excessive alternatives. The poetic muse sees one choice: One Meaningful Experience Now.

- Fragmentation lives now in the past, now in the future, now in the moment, now in the past again, and so on. The poetic muse condenses all time into the pupil of one eye just after its previous blink and prior to its next.

- Fragmentation is filled with pictures, images, symbols, allegories, allusions, metaphors. The poetic muse turns them all into communicable revelations of the human essence and the human process.

In the *Poetics*, when Aristotle discusses art as a *mimesis* (imitation) of life, he is much concerned with a work's unified structure; for only by being an order can it invoke life itself. Thus we read of "beginning, middle and end," and of standard ingredients of plot like the reversal of fortune and unity of action. Though evolving critical theory has deviated from such formal absolutes, the ideal of the unified structure remains a constant.

Emerson has noted the close relationship between nature, order and aesthetics:

The ancient Greeks called the world *kosmos*, beauty. Such

is the constitution of all things, or such the plastic power of the human eye, that the primary forms, as the sky, the mountain, the tree, the animal, give us a delight in and for themselves; a pleasure arising from outline, color, motion, and grouping. (42)

The New Criticism

In discussing a poem as an organized creation that is complete in itself, it is appropriate to refer to the New Critics. "Modern literary study arguably begins with New Criticism" (Lynn 259). It is the New Critics who most approach a work of literature on its own terms, as a self-consistent organism. They see each separate work as a system of discourse, like a language, that creates and resolves its own tensions. The work is a complete world, created by one who, like a deity, says, "Let there be..." New Critics have little interest in the work's "uses" outside of the self-consistent aesthetic experience it creates.

Many critical theories have focused too much on elements extrinsic to the work itself, such as the poet's autobiography, the historical context in which the work was created, or the possible affects the work might have on society. These all have their place, of course. The danger that must be guarded against is one of excess - allowing literature to be little other than a means to some other end.

The line of demarcation has a different location in every theorist's mind. There can be no doubt that my own approach would be considered inappropriate by some on such grounds. The great value of New Criticism is that it reminds all readers of the issue, and encourages them to confront the work primarily as a complete and living system in itself, and *for* itself.

Reflecting all formalistic critical schools and anticipating New Criticism, A.C. Bradley said, in his inaugural lecture as the Oxford Professor of Poetry (1901),

> The consideration of ulterior ends, whether by the poet in the act of composing or by the reader in the act of experiencing, tends to lower poetic value. It does so because it tends to change the nature of poetry by taking it out of its own atmosphere. For its nature is to be not a part, nor yet a copy of the real world...but to be a world by itself, independent, complete, autonomous; and to possess it fully you must enter that world, conform to its laws, and ignore for the time the beliefs, aims, and particular conditions which belong to you in the other world of reality. (Orr 174)

New critic Cleanth Brooks, in a statement that appeared under the title "My Credo: The Formalist Critics" in the Kenyon Review in 1951, presented these "articles of faith"(!):

> That literary criticism is a description and an evaluation of its object. That the primary concern of criticism is with the problem of unity - the kind of whole which the work forms or fails to form, and the relation of various parts to each other in building up this whole...That in a successful work, form and content cannot be separated... (Orr177-8)

So as the New Critics are eager to remind us, a poem requires no use, no justification, other than its own structured life and the interaction of its own components (sounds, rhythms, word denotations and connotations, etc.). By becoming its own organic form, poetry is one way among many that man wages war against the death principle. The poet has not the luxury, as many sometimes seem to, of ignoring the death principle; but at the same time, he is gifted with the ability to transcend it. It becomes merely the context for his orderly creation.

Poetry is a powerful way to create a new world, without violating the a priori world that is shared by all. The seed, the organizing principle for each new world, is the poet's perceiving and formulating mind.

It is worth noting, in passing, that there is a connection here between poetry and schizophrenia, for in each case the mind is presenting to itself its own creation more than some analysis of external reality. However, the work of the poet far surpasses the other in at least three respects:

- Schizophrenia tends to be quite disorderly.

- Poetry represents a grasping of reality in all its joy and horror rather than an avoidance of reality.

- True poetry is not simply peculiar; it is also both beautiful and communicable.

"The force that through the green fuse drives the flower / drives my green age," says Dylan Thomas. "The force that drives the water through the rocks / Drives my red blood." He is vividly conscious, and likewise able to vividly express, the power within him. It is a power that is analogous to

- perhaps even identical with - the most mysterious powers of nature. He is the seed, organizing that amorphous power into his own new creation.

CHAPTER 5

THE RETURN TO CHILDHOOD

> How like an angel came I down!
> How bright are all things here!
> When first among his works I did appear,
> Oh, how their glory did me crown!
> The world resembled his eternity,
> In which my soul did walk;
> And ev'rything that I did see
> Did with me talk.

--Thomas Traherne, "Wonder"

Along with its exhilarations, the process of growing up includes some conspicuous sorrows. Children are filled with energy, wonder and magic, but they often behave in ways that adults find inconvenient, inscrutable, or annoying. Even the best parents will sometimes negate their children unfairly. The small child reverences or fears them, and so automatically accepts negative judgments and unfortunate treatment as legitimate.

Virtually everyone grows up with some degree of self-negation associated with childhood, certainly an important component of the larger human problem. As a result, becoming an adult is not in every way characterized by progress, as both the words "growing" and "up" would seem to imply. Though there are many ways in which adults outperform children, many of the differences are value-neutral, and more than a few of the changes must be characterized as degenerations. These latter changes are doubly tragic because they are largely voluntary. A choice is made to cast off an attitude, activity or personality trait because it has been deemed "childish" or "immature" or "unsophisticated"; and what fills the void - equally a matter of choice - is often nothing more than a caricature of true maturity. There is a tragic confusion of child-LIKE-ness with child-ISH-ness.

Psychologist Alice Miller has brilliantly charted and analyzed this repudiation of one's legitimate childlikeness in her book *The Drama of the Gifted Child*. Significantly, she notes that this "inner child" has not been expunged in most cases. Rather, the child has been locked away in some ignored portion of the psyche. "Probably everybody has a more or less concealed inner chamber that he hides even from himself and in which the props of his childhood drama are to be found" (25). Stefan Kanfer expressed it more passionately: "Inside every man there is a poet who died young" (qtd. in

Peter 406).

An element of literature often neglected by the academic world is its unique role in the lives of adults as a link with legitimate childlikeness. The power of stories and poems in the lives of children is a cliché. What is perhaps not so celebrated is the analogous power that remains throughout the reader's life - the power to bring us back to the wide-eyed wonder of childhood.

Literature and its cognates are for many the only place left to be carefree, or small and helpless, or afraid of the dark and its monsters, or amazed, or unabashedly gleeful. Indeed, it is this very category of experiences that keep the storybooks closed in some households. The repression of childhood sorrows, the subtle rejection of one's most vulnerable self, is an incalculable force for keeping many away from imaginative literature. Not surprisingly therefore, the same force is an explanation that psychologists use in accounting for the rejection of the therapeutic process by many who would benefit from it. Likewise is the unwillingness to "become as a little child" an obstacle to Christians who would otherwise enter more deeply into their professed faith. If that "heavenly Father" is not being allowed to heal some of those childhood wounds, then the wounds are certainly keeping that Father at a distance.

We have thus arrived at the least disputable meeting ground, perhaps we should call it a playground, of literature with psychology and the Christian faith. For in each endeavor, there must be a return to childhood. When Jesus spoke of the need to become like children in order to enter the

Kingdom of God (Matt. 18.3), he demonstrated both psychological and literary insight. The Apostle Paul took the matter even further, teaching that the true spirit of Christianity is to actually call God "Daddy" (*abba*, Gal. 4.6).

The psychotherapeutic process is notorious for its concentration on childhood, and for its insistence that profound understanding and healing often takes place with reference to the past.

Henry Moore describes in his memoirs how, as a small boy, he massaged his mother's back with an oil to soothe her rheumatism. Reading this suddenly threw light for me on Moore's sculptures: the great, reclining women with the tiny heads - I now could see in them the mother through the small boy's eyes, with the head high above, in diminishing perspective, and the back close before him and enormously enlarged. This may be irrelevant for many art critics, but for me it demonstrates how strongly a child's experiences may endure in his unconsciousness and what possibilities of expression they may awaken in the adult who is free to give them rein. (A. Miller 4)

Primary among a man's methods of ignoring his own inner life is the practice of pretension, that is, the covering up of childlike vulnerability with a false show of the contrary characteristics. Thus may an embarrassed or remorse-stricken person make a show of extreme self-confidence; a person who feels weak and helpless finds an even weaker person that he can somehow control; a person who feels incompetent will seek to find one area of extreme competence and then invest his whole life in the practice of that one activity. There are few behaviors in man that separate him more from that which can transform and ennoble him.

The power of poetry, including the fictional, humorous and dramatic forms which it takes, is that it can circumvent pretension and lead out - here cautiously referring again to Aristotle's *psychagogia* - the real, inner person, which includes the lost child who wants once again to be curious and creative.

A poem is a playground, and that perhaps before it is anything else. It is a safe place for adults to play with matters of the greatest gravity. Robert Frost provided a valuable clue when he spoke of "the pleasure of taking pains." The paradox here is simply verbal. Frost meant precisely what the German critic Baumgarten meant when he spoke of the central impulse toward poetry (and toward all art) as the *Spieltrieb*, the play impulse. (Ciardi 5)

From one side, a poem has majesty and power. From the other side it seems so trivial as to be hardly worthy of attention. In being both overlooked and majestic, the poem is just like a child. To peruse one is no more than a childish game, but as the Duke of Wellington colorfully remarked, "the battle of Waterloo was won on the playing fields of Eton." The reader-playmate becomes more substantial and formidable during this game.

Because of this inherent link with childhood, the poet often expresses himself in a manner comparable to a child who is just learning to use language, or in the way man in his earliest history first began to communicate verbally. Says Emerson, "Children and savages use only nouns or names of things, which they convert into verbs, and apply to analogous mental acts" (49). Herein is the wellspring of poetic "techniques" such as onomatopoeia, neologisms, rhythm, rhyme, hyperbole, metonymy, synecdoche, repetition, assonance and dissonance. The connection of such "techniques" with the verbalizations of children is unmistakable. Ironically then, much sophisticated poetical theory seems to represent the efforts of "grown-ups" to account for the genius of children. Such an accounting is right and appropriate, so long as it is never made to take the place of the thing itself. True maturity is never incongruous with the eternal glories of childlikeness, for "infancy is the perpetual Messiah, which comes into the arms of fallen men, and pleads with them to return to paradise." (Emerson 77)

CHAPTER 6

THE SUSPENSION OF DISBELIEF

...(now the ears of my ears awake and
now the eyes of my eyes are opened)

--e. e. cummings, "i thank You God..."

One of the major poetical works appearing in the nineteenth century was the *Lyrical Ballads* of William Wordsworth and Samual Taylor Coleridge. In a later work, the *Bibliographia Literaria*, Coleridge had occasion to describe the original plan of the earlier work. He said this about his own role:

It was agreed, that my endeavors should be directed to persons and characters supernatural, or at least romantic; yet so as to transfer from our inward nature a human interest and a semblance of truth sufficient to procure for these shadows of imagination that willing suspension of disbelief for the moment, which constitutes poetic faith. (Bate 376)

What warrants special consideration here are the phases "suspension of disbelief" and "poetic faith." It is well worth considering what difference, if any, there is between "poetic faith" and "religious faith". For that matter, one may add "psychotherapeutic faith" to the inquiry. The commonalities of poetic and religious faith are even implied by Coleridge himself in the passage immediately following the one just quoted. While delineating the effect that Wordsworth's poems were expected to have on the reader, he invokes biblical teachings concerning unbelief and faith:

Mr. Wordsworth, on the other hand, was to propose to himself as his object, to give the charm of novelty to things of every day, and to excite a feeling analogous to the supernatural, by awakening the mind's attention from the lethargy of custom, and directing it to the loveliness and the wonders of the world before us; an inexhaustible treasure, but for which, in consequence of the film of familiarity and selfish solicitude, we have eyes, yet see not, ears that hear not, and hearts that neither feel nor understand. (Bate 376)

The enticement to "suspend disbelief" in a literary context, is really an invitation to the reader to lay aside his own habitual perceptive grid for a time, in order to try on another - the point of view of a literary work. If the reader clings too zealously to his ordinary belief system - if he is unable to temporarily release himself from the "real world" *as he perceives it* - then many elements of the literary experience will be lost to him. The point of view of a story and the voice of a poem are the places where poet and reader unite. If the reader is to experience the full benefits of the literary enterprise, he must in a very literal sense *believe* in the story. He must share its viewpoint, "try it on"; must briefly hold its metaphysical assumptions; must willingly project some significant portion of his psyche into the work; must trust the author, or at least - to paraphrase Coleridge - forget to distrust him.

It is the author's responsibility to make these shifts as easy as possible for the reader. This is another context in which literary technique must circumvent rational analysis and psychological defense mechanisms, and "trick" the reader - through vivid details, convincing metaphors and muscular language - into experiencing its own reality rather than objectively observing the action. The reader must, for a moment, lose objectivity.

In the New Testament, the words "faith" and "believe" are merely two English translations of the same Greek root - *pistis* and *pisteuo*). With this in mind, the phrase "suspension of disbelief" becomes employable as a colorful and insightful way of referring to religious faith. The word "faith" has religious connotations; "belief" usually does not. Nevertheless, the denotation is identical. What the God of the Bible invites his hearers to do is to share his "point of view" of the human experience, the human story; and to "hear his voice."

It is required of the psychiatric patient, with trust, to "try on" some new perceptions as he goes through the therapeutic process. The psychologist acts very much like a poet, creating living stories - perceptive alternatives - and inviting the patient to step into them.

It is assumed that dysfunctionality in daily life largely stems from unconsciously projecting one's own harmful, repressed psychic matter on to the various people and events of everyday affairs. One of the most stirring experiences available to the patient is the discovery of just how much a seeming "reality" is subject to change, because his perceptions of "reality" have been chosen - usually unconsciously, usually in response to childhood pressures - among a host of alternatives. Perceptions of reality, far from having the objectivity that is usually assumed, are to a significant degree projected; or, to coin a term, faithed. And one's faith, one's projection, one's point of view, is alterable. In the psychotherapeutic process, this modification of one's inward perceptions is seen as both easier than, and preferable too, endlessly struggling with external realities over which one may have little control.

So the psychiatric patient is led to a new set of perceptions-faiths-points of view by confronting his habitual set and being challenged in a new direction. The listener to Paul's preaching is led to new perceptions-faiths-points of view about his life, based on the idea of a God who expresses his nature in the personality and actions of Jesus. The reader of good literature gives himself over to unusual and powerful perceptions-faiths-points of view that can alter forever his understanding of himself and life in general.

CHAPTER 7

THE ROLE OF THE DREAM

All that we see or seem
Is but a dream within a dream.

-Edgar Allan Poe, "A Dream within a Dream"

The centrality of dream analysis to Freudian and Jungian psychology is widely known. Its importance arises from the conviction, rooted in extensive therapeutic experience and research, that dreams are efforts on the part of the subconscious to communicate itself to consciousness.

In the early days of psychoanalysis, the most important aid to clinical procedure was the interpretation of dreams. The book with that title remains one of the most widely read of Freud's works and the basis of more than one theory of poetry and the imagination.

> The advantage of the dream over the active but conscious association of ideas in the analyst's office should be obvious. Freud early claimed that the interpretation of dreams was "the via regia to the interpretation of the unconscious, the surest ground of psychoanalysis and a field in which every worker must win his convictions and gain his education." Why should this be so? Because the dream state illustrates clearly, and without the usual handicaps to reliability, "the processes occurring in the deeper, unconscious layers of the mind, which differ considerably from the familiar normal processes of thought." The function of the dream is to induce and to prolong sleep. It is a condition in which the psychic self renounces the external world, and the principle of reality that dominates it. (Hoffman 10-11)

Once again, there are provocative comparisons to be made here, once one looks beyond the specialized terminology, with the dream experiences described in the Bible. No dream is ever reported there that does not have profound psycho-spiritual application to the dreamer. To borrow the language of the above quotation, biblical dreams are, without exception, communications that intrude upon "the external world, and the principle of reality which dominates it." They reveal what is normally hidden, and God himself is very often named as the revealer. Intriguing examples may be found in Gen. 28.10-17 and Matt. 2.13.

A dream is a purely mental experience that is perceived as a primarily bodily experience. Here then is a crossing over of existential categories. We generally think of human experiences as primarily involving the body. Skydiving is exhilarating and sometimes frightening because of its danger to the body; lovemaking is a bodily pleasure; even such a simple activity as walking along a busy city boulevard involves a host of bodily connections. People are significantly changed by their experiences largely because of the way bodily interactions influence the inner life. However, the dreamer can be impacted just as significantly even though his sleeping body is as inactive as it can possibly be short of death. This is because the inner life, the personal spirit, is engendering experiences that are as vivid as if they were happening to the body.

These experiences can be deeply profound. In the vocabulary of psychology, they are symbolic communications from the deepest self, or in the case of the collective unconscious, from a depth even deeper than the self. In the vocabulary of the Christian faith, they are prophetic or revelatory.

John Gardner explains the connection to the literary experience. "If we carefully inspect our experience as we read, we discover the importance of physical details... [They create] for us a kind of dream, a rich and vivid play in the mind" (30). Both fiction and poetry, when they work as they should, create something very like a dream state. Outstanding recent examples in fiction are Gabriel Garcia Marquez' *One Hundred Years of Solitude* and Toni Morrison's *Sula*. In poetry, Coleridge's "Ancient Mariner" comes easily to mind; or Henry Reed's "Naming of Parts" - a poetical dream portraying a literal dream.

To speak of a story or poem as a dream is little different than saying it communicates to consciousness the profound dynamics that are typically beneath consciousness. It is also little different than saying it carries prophetic communications from the realm of the "supernatural." How is this accomplished? First and most importantly, good literature always circumvents the mind's tendency to control experience through rational analysis. To fully experience something is to not yet understand it. In the existential moment, there is a sense of being or doing rather than understanding, or there is no self-consciousness whatever. There are conflicting attitudes or responses, paradoxes, cognitive dissonances. One feels anticipation and challenge. Understanding may come later, but a poem is a picture, an image, a performance, not an explanation. It is action, movement, sound, physical sensation, taste, scent. It awakens the senses, creating the "body-ness" which is essential to full apprehension.

All poetic experiences have this is common: They are subtle anticipations of some culmination of human progression and growth. Or, less commonly, they are a tragic portrayal of the failure to progress. In either case, there is an immeasurable sadness in poetic experience as we become connected to the deepest sources of our imperfection; there is a longing for our fullest glory, an exhilaration as we dimly see our way to the goal, and a strengthening to face the obstacles with courage. All these experiences are dreamlike, obscure to ordinary waking consciousness, precisely because they are events that are happening in one's personal, inward essence.

CHAPTER 8

HELPERS AND ANTAGONISTS

All houses wherein men have lived and died
    Are haunted houses...

--Henry Wadsworth Longfellow, "Haunted Houses"

In a brilliant essay on Henry James' *The Turn of the Screw*, Robert Heilman offers the following interpretations:

I am convinced that, at the level of action, the story means exactly what it says:

...At Bly there are apparitions which the governess sees, which Mrs. Grose does not see but comes to believe in because they are consistent with her own independent experience, and of which the children have a knowledge which they endeavor to conceal...Mrs. Grose...is the commonplace mortal, well intentioned, but perceiving only the obvious; the children are the victims of evil, victims who, ironically, practice concealment - who doubtless must conceal - when not to conceal is essential to salvation. (284)

Later in the same essay (p. 288), Heilman states that within Bly are "echoes of the Garden of Eden." Heilman's comments refer, in these brief portions of his essay, to a number of the themes that I have discussed in previous chapters of this book: children and innocence, concealment and ordinary levels of awareness, salvation and ideal states. However, the focus of the present chapter will be on that range of human experiences which is brought to mind by his use of the word, "apparitions."

Etymologically, the word apparition is related to the word "appearance," and can refer generally to the act of becoming visible, especially if such appearing is unexpected. It is in this connection that the word takes on its ghostly or spiritual connotations.

Whitley Strieber, the modern writer of science fiction and related stories, published in 1987 a book entitled *Communion* in which he described as factual his numerous experiences with some "apparitions." What raises *Communion* above the level of mere genre fiction is its author's singularly studious and intelligent attempts to analyze his experience and to find an appropriate category for his visitors.

He discusses at some length the explanation that they represent some "trick of the mind," and he summarizes his investigations into a condition known as Temporal Lobe Disorder. He entertains the possibility that the experiences are particularly realistic dreams, or that the visitors come from somewhere in distant space. Ideas of the angelic and demonic arise. He acknowledges the fact that he has a very powerful imagination, and that various childhood fantasies may have some kind of peculiar hold on him. He even connects the sort of experiences that may have led to the ancient belief in a pantheon of gods.

Strieber draws no conclusions, and his inconclusiveness may be the most compelling element of the book, for it leaves one open to a somewhat startling speculation: Is it possible that some or all of these explanations have a certain validity all at the same time? Is it possible that each is explaining, from its own perspective, the same category of experiences? Is it possible for one event to be at once a "trick of the mind," a dream, a fantasy, an alien visitation, and a connection to the supernatural realm? Why must our categories be so inflexible? Why not let them mingle?

Peck's *People of the Lie* describes a number of chilling clinical experiences that altered his views on the supernatural from scientific skepticism to unquestioning belief in a literal devil.

James Friesen, another psychologist, has contributed an even more disturbing study in his *Uncovering the Mystery of MPD*. This book is a psychological, sociological and religious study of the condition known as Multiple Personality Disorder, "the existence within an individual of two or more distinct personalities, each of which is dominant at a particular time" (Friesen, 43). Among the many unusual contributions of this study is the documenting of a connection between MPD and the ritual abuse of children. There is also an attempt to chart gradations of severity among MPD sufferers, and MPD's relation to the demonic.

Of course, the everyday work of the psychologist is not usually concerned with such odd and controversial possibilities. Rather, that work is concerned with differing "ego states," fragments of the psyche, and what are referred to as introjects. An introject, mentioned frequently in Alice Miller's work, may be defined as a mental image or voice, often of an actual person, that has been unconsciously incorporated into the psyche. One's parents are the most common introjected entities. Once in the psyche, the introject can have quite an impact, even "speaking into" an individual's thoughts and ideas.

It is an intriguing question, one well worth considering: To what degree may parallels be drawn between the above religious and psychological phenomena and the limitless variety of "characters" in imaginative literature - the famously memorable characters of Dickens, for example? What is the seemingly infinite source of these characters? In addition, what is the nature of their "existence"? The simplest answer is to say that they are "imaginary," but hopefully, having reached this point, such an explanation will seem inadequate. What if the imagination is more a way of seeing than a way of inventing? What if it is both at the same time?

It is a rather banal observation that authors draw their characters from real life, but it is made less so when the phrase real life encompasses a genuine realm which brings together introjects, alter personalities, spirits and mythical gods; a transcendent world which comes to us in apparitions. The description transcendent here would have reference more to our failure to understand, than to some inherent superiority of another realm.

John Ciardi, probably never dreaming to what extremes his words might be taken, introduced his book on the meaning of poetry in this way:

It is true that every good poem stirs random private associations. The words, images, rhythms, forms, and dramatic situations of good poems are haloed by ghosts, and the ability to release them is perhaps the basic source of poetic power. Still nothing will direct a reader to the experience of a poem until he sees that the ghosts of a poem talk to one another. The "ghost" (aura, connotation, suggestion, overtone) of every formal element arises in response to the other ghosts of the poem. This book is about such ghosts, and about the poet's techniques for entrapping them and for directing their conversation to one another... (xx-xxi)

One literary example is especially worth mentioning in this connection because of its special application to the Christian Faith. In Shakespeare's Othello, the tragic plot is driven by the actions of Iago, an extraordinarily malevolent, devious, and brilliantly conceived character. His personality and motivations, his ultimate goals and intermediate objectives, his manner and methodologies, should all be of the utmost interest to the believing student of the Bible.

It is arguable that one who has an interest in the devil - whether literal, figurative or literary - can find him portrayed more in the character of Iago than in any theological work including the Bible itself. It would only aid the devout Christian's competence in spiritual endeavor to observe a literary devil at work: the subtleties, the seemingly minor manipulations of people and circumstances, the well-timed suggestions, the half-truths, the hidden agendas, the posing and posturing, the deceptive kindnesses. Must the wisdom of such a work be taken lightly simply because it comes from Shakespeare rather than the Holy Scriptures? Each of us will answer that question for himself.

Acknowledging the Helpers

More than one student of Paradise Lost has noticed how much more interesting and substantial Milton's diabolic characters are than those who adhere to righteousness, with Satan himself being the most interesting of all. And Paradise Lost is by no means the only work in which this is so. There seems to be a psychological and literary principle at work here that what is malfunctioning and requires fixing commands more attention than that which behaves as it should. The matter can be illustrated by shoes that do, and shoes that do not, fit. The former are comfortable to the one walking in them, and thus receive little attention.

I have clearly followed this tendency in the execution of this chapter, writing exclusively of the "antagonists" and completely ignoring the "helpers" of our psycho-spiritual-literary journey. So it must be observed, in concluding the chapter, that the transcendent realm, in addition to its villains, is replete with various allies and heroes. There are introjects that nurture and defend. There are angels, core personalities, "wise men", holy spirits and saviors. And literature has the power to invoke them all, now in the guise of the "Goodly Fere," now as Touchstone or Horatio, now as a hunchback with a tragically loyal and beautiful soul.

Perhaps that condition which psychology calls wholeness and which Christianity calls holiness, can satisfactorily be described as an "inner dialogue" wherein characters such as these have gained prominence.

CONCLUSION

Carl Jung articulated well the contrast between the transcendent and the temporal:

Life has always seemed to me like a plant that lives on its own rhizome. Its true life is invisible, hidden in the rhizome. The part that appears above ground lasts only a single summer. Then it withers away - an ephemeral apparition. When we think of the unending growth and decay of life and civilization, we cannot escape the impression of absolute nullity. Yet I have never lost a sense of something that lives and endures underneath the eternal flux. What we see is the blossom, which passes. The rhizome remains. (Memories 4)

The three disciplines treated in this book have common elements because each engages, each from its own vantage point, the identical realm. This realm - non-material, eternal, represented to ordinary consciousness through symbols - has been described here as both primary and transcendent. It has been contrasted with the secondary, temporal realm perceived by ordinary waking consciousness.

The secondary realm, the means by which consciousness veils and mediates the totality of spiritual reality, is mainly material, and largely subject to our perceptive choices. As an object of personal experience, it is undeniably transient, but in the midst of this transient realm, a lengthy and wide-ranging series of decision-making opportunities is presented to every individual human psyche.

True human growth and development involves a gradual release from the temporal realm and from the body and conventional perceptions that function within that realm. Coinciding with this gradual release is an increasing acquaintance and comfort with, and competence in, the transcendent. Every conscious or unconscious decision of the individual is ultimately a response to the call of this process. The process is very comparable to a journey whose destination is both self-discovery and self-definition. The journey takes place in both realms at the same time, the secondary providing a reflection to ordinary consciousness of what is taking place in the primary.

The transcendent lies behind, within, and throughout all that is commonplace, and inspires all experiences that can be properly labeled psychological, spiritual, religious, poetic, mythical, subconscious, para-rational, paranormal or imaginative. Even much that is called by the name of fantasy is, in fact, a literal and eventually undeniable reality. Religion, psychology and the literary experience all claim, each in its own way, that there is nothing so present, so real, and so lasting as that which is "only in our minds."

One of the greatest and most tragic errors of the present age is its failure to see that if something exists "only in the mind," it exists. At some time early in their lives, most people unconsciously make the decision to separate bodily experiences from purely mental experiences and to regard experiences that include the body as somehow more "real" than the other. But this separation is artificial, even deceptive. If we define "real" as meaning nothing more than "involving the body," then we have said nothing significant about human experience; we have only shown how we use words. However, ideas, fantasies, imaginings are inside our minds and affect us in no less significant a manner than people and money and cars and mountains enter our minds and affect us. There is no such thing as "just a story," unless we can also use with comfort a phrase like "just the weather" or "just a dental appointment." Dreams, physical objects, fears, checkbooks, smells, memories, animals: they are all made of the same "stuff" once they have been ingested by the mind. Whatever meaning or significance the external world has to us is a meaning that exists nowhere else than in the human mind.

The artificial division between physical experience ("real") and mental experience ("imagined") is the result of what the Judeo-Christian tradition calls the fall. Throughout the Scriptures, man is said to be separated, and what he is most separated from is the literal reality of that which he habitually considers imaginary and therefore inconsequential.

One may well ask why, beyond the author's mere personal preference, Christianity was chosen for this synthesis over other systems of religious symbolism - which admittedly would be equally subject to the same kind of synthesis. C. S. Lewis answers this question eloquently in his essay, "Myth Became Fact," pointing out the very unique connection between Christ and the pursuit of literature:

> The heart of Christianity is a myth which is also a fact. The old myth of the Dying God, without ceasing to be myth, comes down from the heaven of legend and imagination to the earth of history. It happens - at a particular date, in a particular place, followed by definable historical consequences. We pass from a Balder or an Osiris, dying nobody knows when or where, to a historical Person crucified (it is all in order) under Pontius Pilate. By becoming fact it does not cease to be myth: that is the miracle. I suspect that men have sometimes derived more spiritual sustenance from myths they did not believe than from the religion they professed... A man who disbelieved the Christian story as fact but continually fed on it as myth would, perhaps, be more spiritually alive than one who assented and did not think much about it. (66)

It is a tragedy when preoccupation with the secondary realm as an end in itself keeps human beings from purposefully developing their transcendent natures. We seem to be made for transcendence. Our bodies and our symbolic systems (language, mathematics, science, etc.) are tools which allow us to shield ourselves from that destiny to whatever degree such shielding is necessary at a given moment. But we are or should be in that process of half-discovering, half-creating a godlike ("godly") self; godlike not only in that word's narrow moral sense, but in its full range of meaning: godlike wisdom, competence, self-sufficiency and power, happiness, kindness, and even godlike playfulness. Indeed, we may be involved in a secret process of helping to define godlikeness. It must be a lengthy process because it must involve our own decisions, our own will.

That process spends its first eighty or so years in what we know as the material and social universe, the world of sunlight, wind, oceans, houses, jobs, families, conflicts, crimes, hopes, regrets. It is a world of evolutions and entropies. It is a world of time, space and change precisely because it must give mankind an infinite number of contexts in which to decide exactly what sort of entity a "mankind" is going to be.

Advocates of each of the three enterprises herein examined are sometimes over-eager to distinguish their favorite from the other two, but surely there is an underlying unity beneath those disagreements and conflicts. Perhaps this book can serve as an advancement in human progress by showing at least two additional sources of vital experience beyond whichever one the reader prefers. There is no need to surrender one to go to another. On the contrary, the experience of literature can only be enhanced by an awareness of its reflection of one's own psychological dynamics; the Christian experience can only be enhanced by reawakening one's literary imagination; and so forth.

When the three are at odds, the issues are almost always matters of seeming content: Theology and the Christian view of man (creationism, absolute truth, original sin, vicarious atonement, biblical authority) struggle with the Freudian or Jungian doctrines (evolutionary theory, relativism, original innocence, complexes, the centrality of sex, parental influence or the collective unconscious). The content of literature only increases the level of conflict (freedom of expression vs. censorship, deconstruction vs. objective meaning, tradition vs. original genius). What I have attempted to demonstrate is that content, significant as it is, is not the fundamental element in any of these endeavors. Beneath the dogmas and theories is a common inward momentum, a common process.

To express it in another way, the three disciplines issue a common call to their devotees, a call more to a mode of being than to any closed belief system. The call is to explore the uncomfortably hidden, to *try on* legitimate childlikeness, trust, healthy circumspection, and orderly creation. To the degree these are engaged in, appropriate beliefs and ideas are certain to follow.

It is the burden of religion, psychology and literature, each in its own way but each restating or supplementing the others' information, to help mankind remember the "world behind the veil"; to demonstrate its reality, lurking subtly behind the little dramas of daily experience; to always be encouraging transitions from ordinary to extraordinary. This is especially the value of the true poets, who have the gift and the curse of excessive sight, and who struggle for the words that will help us share their vision.

WORKS CITED

Abrams, M. H. *Natural Supernaturalism: Tradition and Revolution in Romantic Literature*. New York: W. W. Norton and Company, Inc., 1971.

Aristotle. *Poetics*. Bate 19-39.

Arnold, Matthew. "Dover Beach." *Poems in English 1530- 1940: Edited with Critical Notes and Essays*. Ed. David Daiches. New York: The Ronald Press Company, 1950. 508-9.

Austen, Jane. *Pride and Prejudice. The Penguin Complete Novels of Jane Austen*. London: Penguin Books, 1983. 223-445.

Barfield, Owen. "Dream, Myth, and Philosophical Double Vision." *Myths Dreams, and Religion*. Ed. Joseph   Campbell. Dallas: Spring Publications, Inc., 1970.

Bate, Walter Jackson, ed. *Criticism: The Major Texts*. San Diego: Harcourt Brace Jovanovich, Publishers, 1970.

Bly, Robert. *Iron John: a Book about Men*. Reading, Mass.: Addison-Wesley, 1990.

Bunyan, John. *The Pilgrim's Progress*. London: The Folio Society, 1962.

Byron, George Gordon, Lord. *Manfred: A Dramatic Poem. George Gordon, Lord Byron: Selected Poetry and Letters*, Edited with an Introduction and Notes. Ed. Edward E. Bostetter. New York: Holt, Rinehart and Winston, 1967.

Campbell, Joseph. *The Hero with a Thousand Faces*. Bollingen Series 17; Princeton: Princeton University Press, 1972.

Cassirer, Ernst. *An Essay on Man: An Introduction to a Philosophy of Human Culture*. New Haven: Yale University Press, 1944.

Ciardi, John. *How Does a Poem Mean?* Boston: Houghton Mifflin Co., 1959.

Coleridge, Samuel Taylor. from *Biographia Literaria*. Bate 376-86.

---. "The Rime of the Ancient Mariner." *Immortal Poems of the English Language: An Anthology*. Ed. Oscar Williams. New York: Washington Square Press, 1952. 269-288.

The Complete Grimm's Fairy Tales. New York: Pantheon Books, 1944.

Crane, Stephen. *The Red Badge of Courage: An Episode of the American Civil War*. New York: Avon Books, 1979.

Cummings, E. E. *I: Six Nonlectures*. Cambridge, Massachusetts: Harvard University Press, 1953.

---. "i thank You God for most this amazing." Complete Poems: 1913-1962. San Diego: Harcourt Brace Jovanovich, Publishers, 1980.

Dickens, Charles. *David Copperfield*. Toronto: Bantam Books, 1981.

---. *Great Expectations*. New York: Airmont Books, 1965.

Eliot, T. S. "Journey of the Magi." *Poems in English 1530-1940: Edited with Critical Notes and Essays*. Ed. David Daiches. New York: The Ronald Press Company, 1950. 618-19.

Emerson, Ralph Waldo. "Nature." *Selected Essays, Edited with an Introduction by Larzer Ziff*. New

York: Penguin Books, 1982. 35-82.

---. "The Poet." ibid. 259-284.

Euripides. The Bacchae of Euripides. Trans. Donald
Sutherland. Lincoln: University of Nebraska Press,
1968.

---. *Electra*. Trans. Edward P. Coleridge. Vol. 5 of
Great Books of the Western World. 54 vols. Ed.
Robert Maynard Hutchins. Chicago: Encyclopedia
Britannica, Inc., 1952.

Frazer, James George. *The Golden Bough: A Study
in Magic and Religion; 1 Volume, Abridged Edition*.
New York: Macmillan Publishing Co., Inc. 1963.

Friesen, James. *Uncovering the Mystery of MPD*.
San Bernardino, CA: Here's Life Publishers, Inc.,
1991.

Frost, Robert. "A Considerable Speck." *Modern
American Poetry, Modern British Poetry: A Critical
Anthology*. Ed. Louis Untermeyer. New York:
Harcourt, Brace and Company, 1930. Part 1, 232-
33.

Frye, Northrop. "The Archetypes of Literature."
Bate 601-609.

Gardner, John. *The Art of Fiction; Notes on Craft
for Young Writers*. New York: Vintage Books, 1985.

Heilman, Robert. "The Turn of the Screw as Poem."
Scott 283-301.

Hoffman, Frederick J. *Freudianism and the Literary Mind*. Baton Rouge: Louisiana State University Press, 1957.

The Holy Bible: the Authorized or King James Version of 1611 now reprinted with the Apocrypha. London: The Nonesuch Press, 1963.

Homer. The Iliad and The Odyssey. Trans. Samuel Butler. Vol. 4 of Great Books of the Western World. 54 vols. Ed. Robert Maynard Hutchins. Chicago: Encyclopedia Britannica, Inc., 1952.

Ibsen, Henrik. *The Master Builder*. Trans. Rolf Fjelde. Henrik Ibsen: Four Major Plays. New York: New American Library, 1965.

James, Henry. *The Turn of the Screw*. New York: New American Library, 1962.

Joyce, James. *A Portrait of the Artist as a Young Man*. New York: Penguin Books, 1976.

Jung, C. G. *Memories, Dreams, Reflections*. Ed. Aniela Jaffe. New York: Vintage Books, 1965.

---. "On Synchronicity." The Portable Jung. Ed.
Joseph Campbell. New York: Penguin Books, 1976.
511-512.

Kafka, Franz. *The Metamorphosis*. New York:
Bantam Books, 1972.

Lewis, C.S. "Myth Became Fact." *God in the Dock*.
Ed. Walter Hooper. Grand Rapids, Michigan:
William B. Eerdmans Publishing Co., 1970.

Longfellow, Henry Wadsworth. "Haunted Houses."
Poems. New York: A. L. Burte, 1900. 332-33.

Lynn, Steven. "A Passage into Critical Theory."
College English 52.3 (1990): 258-270.

Marquez, Gabriel Garcia. *One Hundred Years of
Solitude*. 1967. Trans. Gregory Rabassa. New York:
Harper & Row, Publishers, 1970.

Miller, Alice. *The Drama of the Gifted Child; The
Search for the True Self*. New York: Basic Books,
Inc., 1981.

Miller, J. Hillis. *Theory Now and Then*. Durham:
Duke University Press, 1991.

John Milton: *Paradise Lost, Samson Agonistes,*

Lycidas. Ed. Edward Le Comte. New York: New American, 1961.

Mitchell, Stephen. *Tao Te Ching: A New English Version, with Foreword and Notes*. New York: Harper & Row, Publishers, 1988.

Morrison, Toni. *Sula*. 1973. New York: New American Library, 1982.

New American Standard Bible. Chicago: Moody Press, 1960.

Orr, Leonard. *A Dictionary of Critical Theory. New York*: Greenwood Press, 1991.

Peck, M. Scott. *People of the Lie: The Hope for Healing Human Evil*. New York: Simon & Schuster, 1985.

---. *The Road Less Traveled; A New Psychology of Love, Traditional Values and Spiritual Growth*. New York: Simon & Schuster, 1978.

Peter, Laurence J. *Peter's Quotations; Ideas for Our Time*. New York: Bantam Books, 1977.

Plato. *The Republic. Great Dialogues of Plato*. Ed. Warmington, Eric H., and Philip G. Rouse. Trans. W. H. D. Rouse. New York: Mentor, 1956. 118-422.

Poe, Edgar Allan. "A Dream within a Dream." *The Oxford Book of American Verse*. Ed. F. O. Matthiessen. New York: Oxford University Press, 1950. 199-200.

Pound, Ezra. "Ballad of the Goodly Fere." *Immortal Poems of the English Language: An Anthology*. Ed. Oscar Williams. New York: Washington Square ¼Press, 1952. 526.

Polking, Kirk, Joan Bloss and Colleen Cannon, eds. *Writer's Encyclopedia*. Cincinnati, Ohio: Writers' Digest Books, 1983.

Reed, Henry. "Naming of Parts." *Immortal Poems of the English Language: An Anthology*. Ed. Oscar Williams. New York: Washington Square Press, 1952. 604.

Richards, Ivor Armstrong. "Irrelevant Associations and Stock Responses." Bate 575-578.

Robinson, Edwin Arlington. "Mr. Flood's Party." *Selected Poems*. Ed. Morton Dauwen Zabel. New York: Collier Books, 1966.

Scott, Wilbur S. *Five Approaches of Literary Criticism: An Arrangement of Contemporary Critical Essays*. New York: The Macmillan

Company, 1962.

Shakespeare, William. *The Plays and Sonnets*. Ed.
William George Clark and William Aldis Wright.
Vols. 26 and 27 of *Great Books of the Western
World*. 54 vols. Ed. Robert Maynard Hutchins.
Chicago: Encyclopedia Britannica, Inc., 1952.

Shelley, Percy Bysshe. "A Defence of Poetry." Bate
429-4ª35.

---. "Hymn to Intellectual Beauty." *Immortal Poems
of the English Language: An Anthology*. Ed. Oscar
Williams. New York: Washington Square Press,
1952. 269-288.

Sophocles. Oedipus the King. Trans. Richard C.
Jebb. Vol. 5 of *Great Books of the Western World*.
54 vols. Ed. Robert Maynard Hutchins Chicago:
Encyclopedia Britannica, Inc., 1952.

Spengler, Oswald. *The Decline of the West*. 2 vols.
New York: Alfred A. Knopf, 1980.

Strieber, Whitley. *Communion: A True Story*. New
York: Avon Books, 1987.

Terry, Milton S. *Biblical Hermeneutics*. Grand
Rapids, Mich.: Zondervan Publishing House, n.d.

Tennyson, Alfred. "Ulysses." *Poems in English*

1530-1940: Edited with Critical Notes and Essays.
Ed. David Daiches. New York: The Ronald Press
Company, 1950. 447-49.

Thomas, Dylan. "The force that through the green
fuse drives the flower." *The Collected Poems of
Dylan Thomas: 1934-1952*. 1956. New York: New
Direct¼ions Publishing Corporation, 1971. 10.

Traherne, Thomas. "Wonder." *Immortal Poems of
the English Language: An Anthology*. Ed. Oscar
Williams. New York: Washington Square Press,
1952. 154-55.

Viereck, Peter. "Poet." Ciardi 269-70.

Willard, Dallas. *The Spirit of the Disciplines*. San
Francisco: Harper & Row, 1988.

Wolfe, Humbert. "Thrushes." *Modern American
Poetry, Modern British Poetry: A Critical
Anthology*. Ed. Louis Untermeyer. New York:
Harcourt, Brace and Company, 1930. Part 2, 327.

Wordsworth, William. Preface. *Lyrical Ballads*. By
Wordsworth and Samuel Taylor Coleridge. Bate
335-346